JASMINE'S SO FUSSY!

Written by Judith Heneghan
Illustrated by Jack Hughes

WINDMILL
BOOKS ™

New York

Published in 2016 by **Windmill Books**,
An Imprint of Rosen Publishing
29 East 21st Street, New York, NY 10010

Commissioning Editor: Victoria Brooker
Design: Lisa Peacock and Alyssa Peacock

Library of Congress Cataloging-in-Publication Data

Heneghan, Judith.
Jasmine's so fussy! / by Judith Heneghan.
p. cm. — (Dragon school)
Includes index.
ISBN 978-1-4777-5605-8 (pbk.)
ISBN 978-1-4777-5604-1 (6 pack)
ISBN 978-1-4777-5528-0 (library binding)
1. Etiquette for children and teenagers — Juvenile fiction.
2. Dragons — Juvenile fiction. I. Heneghan, Judith, 1965-. II. Title.
PZ7.H437 Ja 2016
395.1—d23

Manufactured in the United States of America
CPSIA Compliance Information: #WS15WM:
For Further Information contact Windmill Books, New York, New York at 1-866-478-0556

CONTENTS

Jasmine was a happy dragon, most of the time.
She knew what she liked,
and she knew what she didn't like.

She liked to sit on her favorite log, for example.
But she didn't like sitting on the grass.

That didn't matter – did it?

One day, Brandon had some exciting news.
"There's going to be a party! Here, this afternoon!
We can help get everything ready!"
"Ooh!" said Noah. "Let's have balloons
and fancy clothes and strawberry cake!"

Jasmine frowned. She liked
parties, but she didn't
like strawberry cake.

First, the dragons decorated the clearing.
They had a bag of colored balloons.
There were green ones and yellow ones
and red ones and blue ones.

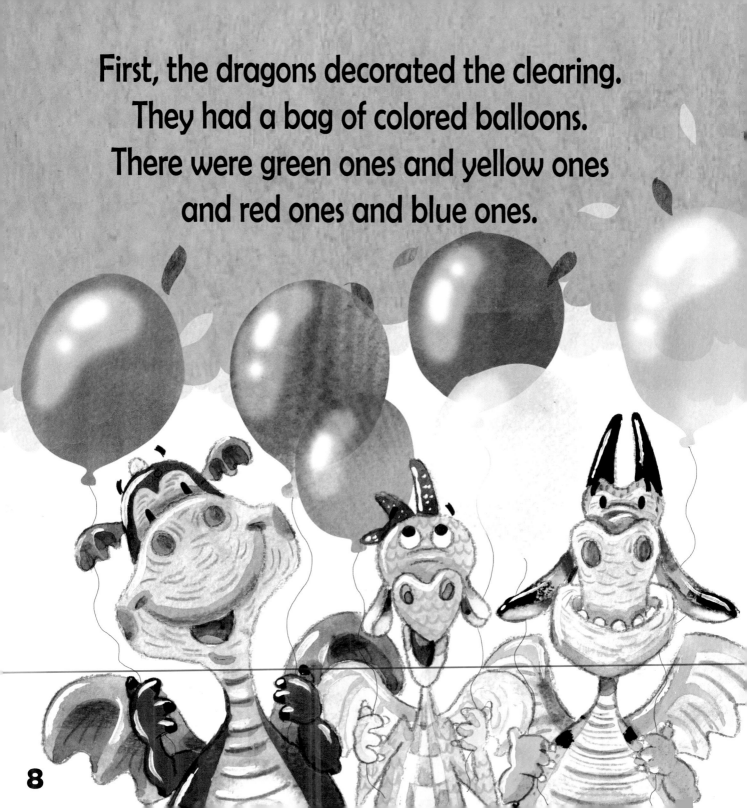

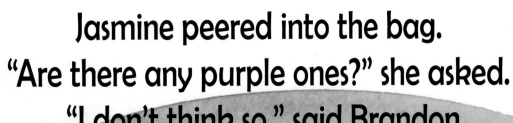

Jasmine peered into the bag.
"Are there any purple ones?" she asked.
"I don't think so," said Brandon,
rummaging. "What about yellow?"

"I don't like yellow," said Jasmine. "I only like purple."

Next, Ruby made a list of party food.
"It's so hard to choose!" she said.
"I love rock burgers and fire cakes
and fruit drops and veggie bites and . . ."

Rock burgers
Fire cakes
Fruit drops
Veggie bites

10

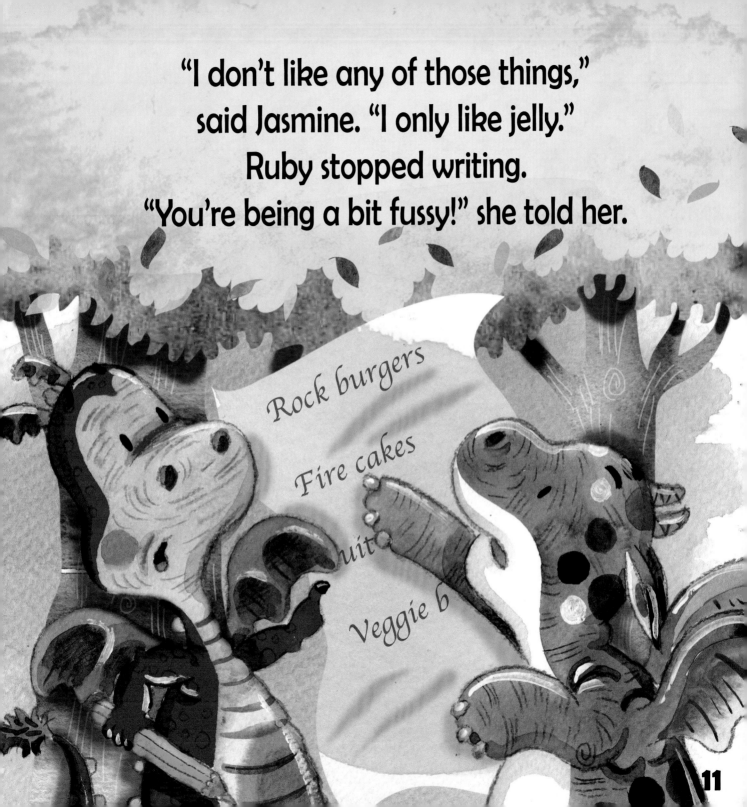

"I don't like any of those things,"
said Jasmine. "I only like jelly."
Ruby stopped writing.
"You're being a bit fussy!" she told her.

Rock burgers

Fire cakes

...uit

Veggie b

11

This gave Brandon an idea.
"Let's pick berries in the forest," he said.
"Then we can make some scrumptious berry jelly!"

But Jasmine trailed behind her friends
as they walked beneath the trees.
She didn't want berries in her jelly.

13

The forest was full of tasty strawberries and juicy blueberries and big green gooseberries. "Wow!" exclaimed Noah. "All this fruit looks amazing!"

14

"Aren't there any purple berries?" asked Jasmine.
"Try a strawberry instead," suggested Brandon.
Jasmine shook her head.
"I won't like it," she said.

15

When the food was ready,
Ruby pulled out the dress-up box.
"What shall I wear?" she wondered.
"This flower necklace or that pirate's hat?"

"I'm going to wear these fancy glasses," said Noah. "What are you going to wear, Jasmine?"

17

Jasmine looked in the box.
"I want to wear a cape," she said,
"but there isn't one."

"Well, here's a feathery scarf," suggested Noah.
"You could wear that.
But you probably don't like feathers."

"No," said Jasmine, sadly.
"I don't."

19

The other dragons were beginning
to feel frustrated.
"You're SO fussy!" said Brandon.
"Being fussy is BORING!" groaned Ruby.
"Why won't you try something DIFFERENT?"
asked Noah.

Suddenly, Jasmine realized she wasn't
looking forward to the party.

21

When the party started, the other dragons
admired the costumes and balloons,
as well as the plates of colorful food.

Jasmine didn't join in.

Jasmine's friends saw her sitting all alone.
She was being a bit silly, but they didn't
want her to feel left out.

So they hatched a plan.

"We've made something for you," said Ruby.
"What is it?" asked Jasmine.
"A surprise," said Brandon.
"You'll have to close your eyes."

"I don't like surprises . . ." wailed Jasmine.
"We think you'll like this one," said Ruby.
Jasmine reluctantly closed her eyes.

Noah brought out the surprise.
Jasmine sniffed.
"That smells nice," she said.

28

"Try some!" urged Brandon.
So Jasmine tried a tiny little bit.
"Mmm!" she said, licking her lips.
"It tastes yummy!" Then she opened her eyes.

29

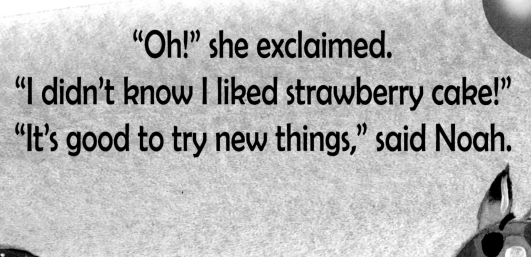

"Oh!" she exclaimed.
"I didn't know I liked strawberry cake!"
"It's good to try new things," said Noah.

"You're right," said Jasmine. "Being fussy IS silly." She grinned. "From now on, I'm going to try EVERYTHING! Let's go and have fun at the party!"

Glossary

frustrated angry, discouraged, or upset because of not being able to do something

hatch to break open or create

reluctant unwilling

rummage to search thoroughly

scrumptious rich or fine, usually describing food

Index

Further Reading

Jeffrey, Gary and Dheeraj Verma. *Dragons*. New York: Gareth Stevens, 2012.

Schneider, Josh. *Very Picky Eaters*. New York: Clarion Books, 2011.

Websites

For web resources related to the subject of this book, go to:
www.windmillbooks.com/weblinks and select this book's title.